Dim Sum for Everyone!

taro

star anise

tapioca

grater

chopsticks

teapot

shrimp

sesame oil

sesame seeds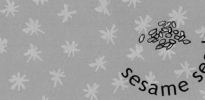

bok choy

carrots

rice vinegar

water chestnuts

coconut milk

sugar

Dim Sum for Everyone!

Grace Lin

DIM SUM

DELL DRAGONFLY BOOKS · NEW YORK

Published by
Dell Dragonfly Books
an imprint of
Random House Children's Books
a division of Random House, Inc.
1540 Broadway
New York, New York 10036

Visit us on the Web! www.randomhouse.com/kids
Educators and librarians, for a variety of teaching tools,
visit us at www.randomhouse.com/teachers

Library of Congress Cataloging-in-Publication Data

Lin, Grace.
Dim sum for everyone! / written and illustrated by Grace Lin.
       p.   cm.
Summary: A child describes the various little dishes of dim sum that she
and her family enjoy on a visit to a restaurant in Chinatown.
ISBN: 0-375-81082-X (trade)
        0-375-91082-4 (lib. bdg.)
        0-440-41770-8 (pbk.)
[1. Dim sum—Fiction. 2. Cookery, Chinese—Fiction.] I. Title.
PZ7.L644 Di 2001
[E]—dc21   00-034813
                                   CIP

Reprinted by arrangement with Alfred A. Knopf

Printed in the United States of America

January 2003

10 9 8 7

To Lissy, who gives my books out at dim sum restaurants

Dim sum has

many little dishes.

Little dishes on carts.

Little dishes on tables.

Ma-Ma picks
little dishes
of sweet pork buns.

Ba-Ba chooses
little dishes
of fried shrimp.

Jie-Jie wants turnip cakes.

Mei-Mei wants
sweet tofu.

I like little egg tarts.

We eat a little

bit of everything.

Everyone eats a

little bit of everything.

Now there are empty little dishes.

Before dim sum became widespread, *yum cha*, or tea drinking, was an important part of Chinese culture. People would visit teahouses after a hard day's labor and socialize with their family members and friends. Teahouses began to serve small dishes of food for customers to snack on while they drank their tea. These small dishes of dumplings, cakes, and buns were called dim sum. Soon dim sum became more popular than the tea!

Dim sum translates many ways. Some translate it as "touches the heart," from "point" (*dim*) and "heart" (*sum*), because customers point and choose whichever dishes their hearts desire. Others believe dim sum means "little heart," because the dishes served are so small.

The dim sum tradition was brought over to the Western world in the mid-19th century. As well as teahouses, we now have busy dim sum restaurants.

There are many little customs of yum cha and dim sum. For instance, when your teapot is empty, leave it open— it's a sign that you need a new pot. To thank the waiter, tap three fingers on the table. And don't worry if the staff doesn't take away your dirty dishes; after your meal is finished, the waiter will count them to calculate your bill!

Families and friends still crowd into dim sum restaurants all over the world. There, amid the rolling trolleys and the bustling atmosphere, people talk, gossip, and share, just as they did so many years ago.

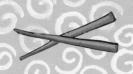

steamed shrimp dumplings

ha gow

crescent dumplings

ham sui gok

stuffed eggplant

yeun ngai guo

fried shrimp

tsi ma ha

coconut pudding cubes

yei tsup go

steamed dumplings

fun gor

turnip cakes

lor bak go

sweet tofu

dao fu fai

rice noodles

cheung fun

sweet pork buns

cha siu bao

steamed meatballs

ngao yuk

thousand-layer cake

tseen tsun go

chicken bundles

gai tsat

almond gelatin

hung yan daofu

sticky rice in lotus leaf

nor my gai

spring rolls

chun guen

pork dumplings

siu my

egg tarts

dan taht

taro dumplings

wu gok

sweet sesame rice balls

jin dui

coconut tapioca

yei tsup sai mailo

stuffed peppers

yeun tsen tsiu